The Gift of GRACE

by Grace Mary McClelland

illustrated by Nancy Moskovitz

Wild Onion Press

BOOKS STARRING KIDS WITH
PHYSICAL DIFFERENCES

Book Design by Walton Dale   www.designwellstudio.com

Illustrations by Nancy Moskovitz

First printing

ISBN 978-1-4507-5218-3, Library of Congress Control Number 2010933222

Printed in the United States using environmentally friendly materials

A portion of the proceeds of this book will be donated to Hands To Love Camp.

Wild Onion Press

BOOKS STARRING KIDS WITH
PHYSICAL DIFFERENCES

12808 N.W. 56 Ave.
Gainesville, Florida 32653

352-213-5740

www.wildonionpress.com

The Gift of
GRACE

by Grace Mary McClelland
illustrated by Nancy Moskovitz

Hello!
My name is
Grace.

I am five years old.
I have blonde hair, green eyes, and some
freckles across my nose.

I love to
sing and dance.

I am a
whiz at puzzles.

I have a beautiful smile.
(That's what my daddy always says.)
My mommy says I'm cheeky.
She's right. We sure have fun!

I have a twin brother.
His name is Patrick.
He often reminds everyone that
he is one minute older than I am.

I also have a special hand.
The fingers on my right hand are much smaller
than the fingers on my left hand.
And instead of five fingers, I have four!
I'm not really sure why I have a special hand.
No one knows for sure.

We know only that I've had this special hand
since I was growing in my mommy's belly.
The doctors have some ideas, but they are only guesses.
Clearly, something stopped my hand from growing
when I was a tiny baby inside my mother.
No one knows WHAT.
And no one knows WHY.

It does not matter.

Having a special hand—a small hand—
makes me different.
All people have differences.
Patrick wears glasses.
That makes him different.

Sometimes I get frustrated when people stare
at my special hand.
Or when they say something unkind.
Once a boy at preschool said,
"You're stupid because you have a stupid little hand."
I think he didn't know how smart I am.
(Nobody has beaten me at the Memory Game!
Not even adults!)
He didn't understand that long fingers
don't make a person smart.
So I explained it to him.

Another time, some girls said I couldn't
play with them because I had a small hand.
Sometimes I feel bad when people say hurtful things.
But usually I try to help them understand
that I can do almost anything other kids do—
even with my special hand.

Of course having a small hand
does mean that I make some choices.
For example, some dolls have tiny little
shoes that are hard for
my special hand to put on
their tiny little feet.
So, I prefer to play with dolls
who have big feet!

I'm learning to make good granny knots.
But it's easier for me to wear shoes
that have no shoelaces—or buckles.
Then there is no need to tie knots.

I love to color, so I've learned to use my left hand,
even though I'm naturally right-handed.
Sometimes my brothers (I have four of them!)
are glad I have a special hand.
When something gets stuck in a small place,
my little hand can get it out.

I have a hand doctor.
He has taken care of me since I was a baby.
He knows a lot about hands.
Every year I see him for a check-up.
He takes pictures of my hand with an X-ray machine.
We talk about how my hand is growing and
how well I am using it.
He is sometimes surprised by how strong my
little hand is.

My doctor has done surgery on my special hand
three times.
You're not going to believe this!
He took some pieces of bone from my toes
and put them in my hand.
That's how I grew little fingers.
How cool is that?
And you can't really tell when you look at my toes,
which, by the way, I love to polish!

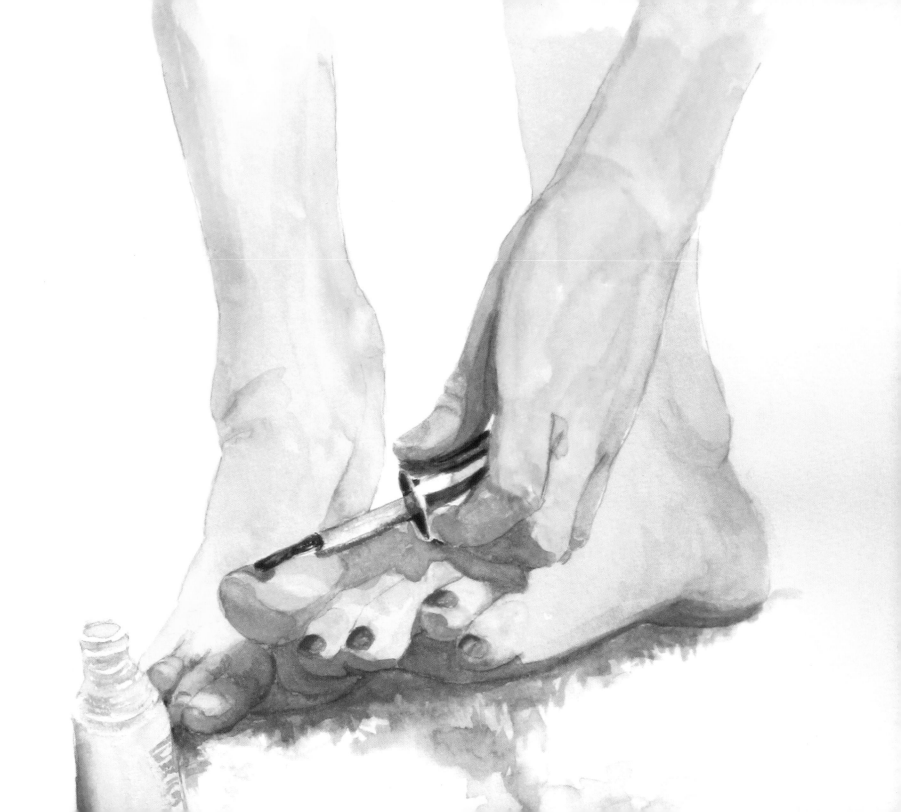

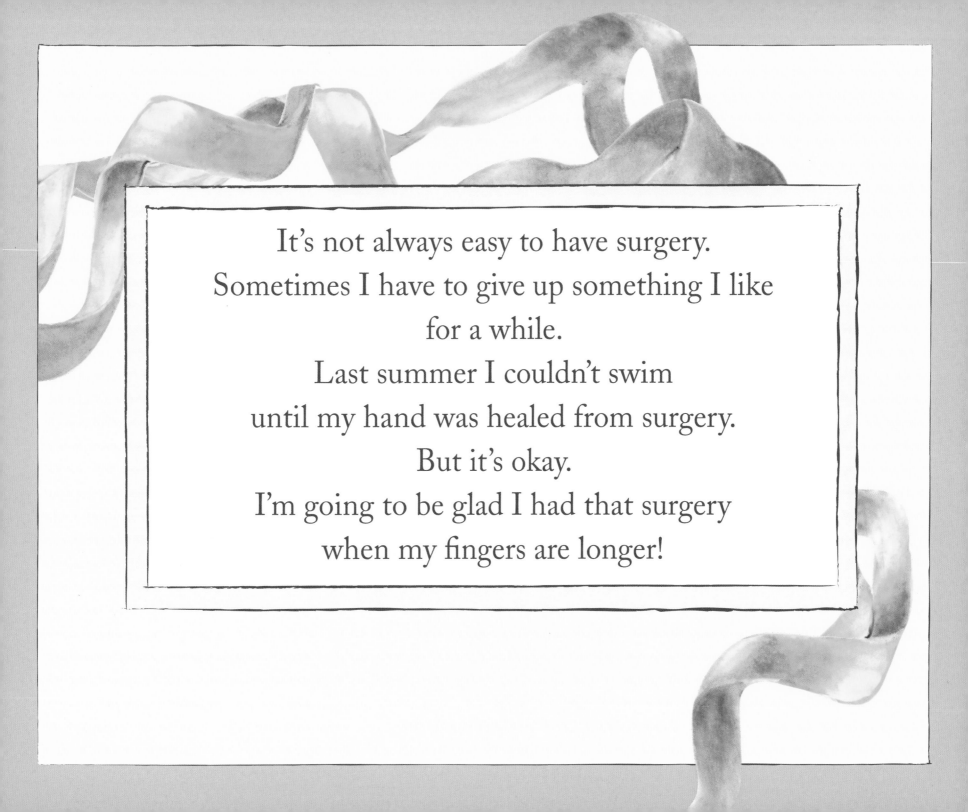

It's not always easy to have surgery.
Sometimes I have to give up something I like
for a while.
Last summer I couldn't swim
until my hand was healed from surgery.
But it's okay.
I'm going to be glad I had that surgery
when my fingers are longer!

The best part of having a special hand is that
I can feel with it.
I put my special hand on my mommy's cheek,
and I feel the love coming through.
Yes, I have a special hand.
It doesn't change the fact that
I am very loving and loveable.

My special hand
is my special gift.

It's the way
I was wonderfully made.

photo: Gayle Fedele

About the Author

Grace wrote this story when she was five.

Inspired, after a preschool classmate commented that she must be stupid because she had a stupid little hand, she told her mother she needed to "set him straight."

"Write this down," she told her mother. "We need to make a book so kids will know what it's like to have a special hand. Most kids know not to make fun of big differences like being blind or in a wheelchair, but they make fun of little things like short fingers or glasses. We need to help them understand."

Over the next weeks, Grace dictated her story.

Today she is an active, beautiful nine-year-old who still enjoys dancing, playing with her brothers, gardening, reading, and writing even more stories to "help people understand." She finds purpose and peace in sharing her gift of grace.

About the Illustrator

Best known for her landscapes and portraits, Nancy Moskovitz is featured in the 2010 edition of *Best of America Watermedia Artists*, Vol. II, by Kennedy Publishing Co. In 2011 The Florida Museum of Natural History is exhibiting the art inspired by her 2007 artist-in-residency on Sapelo Island, GA. Her work hung in the Appleton Museum's Biennial Exhibit in 2006.

Moskovitz earned a BA with honors in education and art history at Simmons College, Boston, footsteps from Sargent and Monet inspirational masterworks in the Boston museums. She left a 15-year teaching career to paint full-time in 2003.

The art in this book is painted in watercolor, watercolor pencil, pastel pencil, and charcoal on Strathmore Aquarius II watercolor paper.